I WANNA NEW ROOM

KAREN KAUFMAN ORLOFF · ILLUSTRATED BY DAVID CATROW

W9-CEM-925

SCHOLASTIC INC.
New York Toronto London Auckland
Sydney Mexico City New Delhi Hong Kong

No part of this publication may be reproduced, stored in a retrieval system, or transmitted in any form
or by any means, electronic, mechanical, photocopying, recording, or otherwise, without written permission of the publisher.
For information regarding permission, write to G. P. Putnam's Sons, a division of Penguin Young Readers Group,
a member of Penguin Group (USA) Inc., 345 Hudson Street, New York, NY 10014.

ISBN 978-0-545-40108-1

Text copyright © 2010 by Karen Kaufman Orloff.
Illustrations copyright © 2010 by David Catrow.
All rights reserved. Published by Scholastic Inc., 557 Broadway, New York, NY 10012,
by arrangement with G. P. Putnam's Sons, a division of Penguin Young Readers Group,
a member of Penguin Group (USA) Inc. SCHOLASTIC and associated logos are
trademarks and/or registered trademarks of Scholastic Inc.

12 11 10 9 8 7 6 5 4 3 2 1   11 12 13 14 15 16/0

Printed in the U.S.A.   40

First Scholastic printing, September 2011

Text set in Catchup and Tekton Pro
The art was done in pencil and watercolor.

For my editor, Susan Kochan,
who guided me and waited patiently
until I got it right. —K.K.O.

To Dad. You taught me everything I know and am. —D.C.

Dear Mom,

I know you think I should share a room with Ethan now that we have Baby Annie, but here's why I shouldn't. When Ethan sleeps, he sounds like the cat coughing up fur balls. Why can't you move Annie in with you and give me my room back?

Signed,

Your very tired son,

Alex

Dear Alex,
Go bother your father.
Signed,
Your very, VERY tired mother

Dear Dad,
You have no idea what it's like to share a room with Ethan! He sticks crayons up his nose and barks like a walrus! And he snores like Grandpa Ralph. So how about giving me my old room back? Please don't say, "Go bother your mother." Been there. Done that.
        Love,
        Fed-up Alex

Dear Alex,

Sorry we had to move you out of your room, but Annie's a girl, and Mom says girls need privacy to do girl stuff. I'm not sure what that is, but I'm guessing it has to do with hair and makeup.

Love,

Dad

Dear Dad,
Annie is a BABY! She doesn't have any hair. And if she wore makeup, she would drool on it! By the way, did I mention Ethan broke my skateboard and lost my brand-new Captain Creepy action figure? The kid is out of control, Dad.
Love,
Your seriously upset child,
Alex

Dear Alex,

You know four-year-olds are a little careless. You were just like him at that age. Remember when you fell into the cake at Grandma's 60th birthday party? Good thing the candles weren't lit! Why don't you have a heart-to-heart talk with Ethan about respecting your property?

Love,

Dad

Dear Dad,

Thanks for the advice. Now I know exactly how to handle this.

Love,

Your diplomatic son, Alex

P.S. "Diplomatic" was one of my vocabulary words.

Dear Alex,

Do you realize you gave Ethan the side of the room that doesn't have a door? I just found him jumping up and down on his bed, yelling that he can't come out to take his bath because Alex said so. Fix this problem when you get home from soccer practice or else!

Love,

Dad

Dear Dad,

Okay, I told Trampoline Boy he can use the door now. Honestly, Dad, you see what I'm dealing with here? Please give me my room back! I promise I'll keep it really, really clean!

Love,
Neat and tidy Alex

Dear Alex,

Does that include cleaning the iguana's cage? I've noticed an unusual smell coming from that general direction. Just thought I'd mention it.

Love,

Your concerned father

Dear Dad,

Let's not change the subject. Here's the thing. I'm practically grown-up. I wanna new room! Plus, I think I should get rewarded for all the A's I got in school.

Love,

Alex the super student

Dear Alex,

Nice try, but if I remember correctly, you got three B's and one A, and I think the A was in Lunch.

Love,

Dad

Dear Dad,

Even Stinky's dog Lurch has his own room! That dog is treated like a king. He's got six pillows and his own TV. He and Stinky watch cartoons and eat cheesy popcorn every single night. I'm not even asking for a TV. Just one little room.

Love,

Your HUMAN son, Alex

P.S. Stinky got a D in Lunch.

Dear Alex,

No can do.

Love, Dad

P.S. Stinky scares me.

Dear Dad,

It's more than the room. It's the principle of the thing! Why do I, the oldest and most important kid, have to suffer just because you and Mom had another baby? Does that seem fair? I don't think so.

Love,

Your number ONE son, Alex

Dear Alex,

Yes, you are very important to us, but so are your brother and sister. However, you make some good points. A boy your age needs his own space. Maybe we could build you a special place of your own.

Love, Dad

Dear Dad,

Now you're talking! We could add a whole new wing onto the house! I can have my own bathroom with a hot tub, skateboard ramp and bowling alley. What do you say, Dad? Here's a floor plan.

Love,
Alex the architect

Dear Alex,

Slow down there, buddy! We're not gazillionaires. We can't build you a condo. I was thinking of something like a tree house. We can build it together. You won't have to share it with your brother unless you absolutely want to.

Love,

Dad

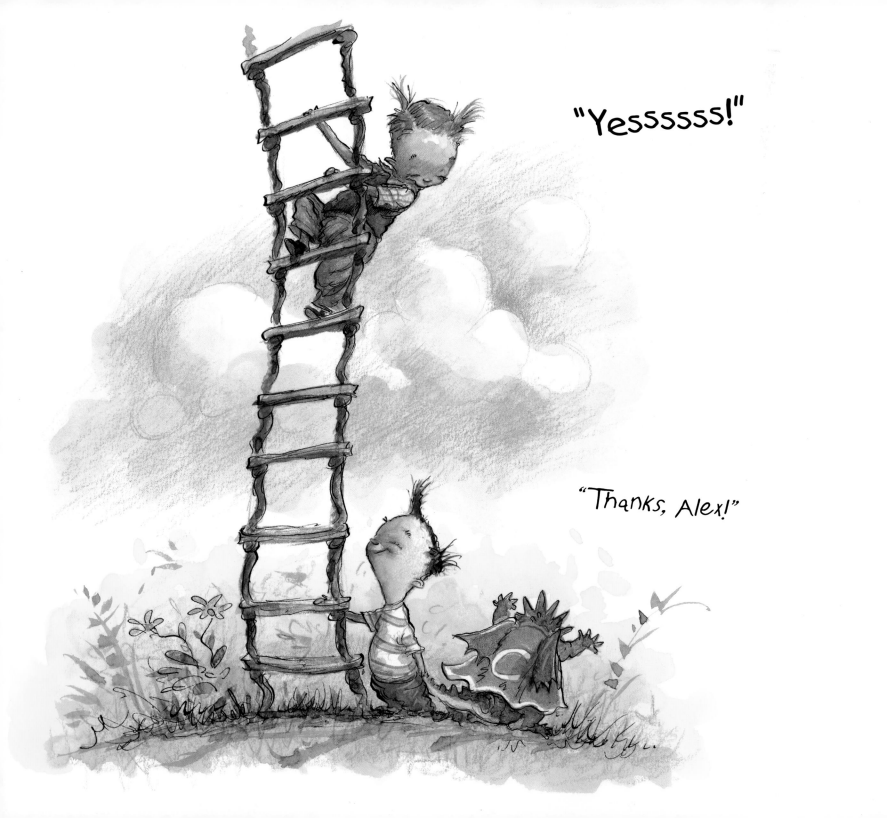